The Tales of
Peter Rabbit and
The Flopsy Bunnies

The reproductions in this book have been made using the most modern electronic scanning methods from entirely new transparencies of Beatrix Potter's original watercolours. They enable Beatrix Potter's skill as an artist to be appreciated as never before, not even during her own lifetime.

FREDERICK WARNE

Published by the Penguin Group
Penguin Books Ltd, 27 Wrights Lane, London W8 5TZ, England
Penguin Books USA Inc., 375 Hudson Street, New York, N.Y. 10014, USA
Penguin Books Australia Ltd, Ringwood, Victoria, Australia
Penguin Books Canada Ltd, 10 Alcorn Avenue, Toronto, Ontario, Canada M4V 3B2
Penguin Books N.Z. Ltd, 182-190 Wairau Road, Auckland 10, New Zealand

The Tale of Peter Rabbit first published 1902
The Tale of The Flopsy Bunnies first published 1909
This compiled edition first published 1995

ISBN 07232 4278 X

PRINTED IN BELGIUM BY

INTERNATIONAL BOOK PRODUCTION

THE TALES OF PETER RABBIT AND THE FLOPSY BUNNIES

THE ORIGINAL AND AUTHORIZED EDITIONS BY

BEATRIX POTTER™

F. WARNE & Co.

THE TALE OF PETER RABBIT

They lived with their Mother in a sand-bank, underneath the root of a very big fir-tree.

'Now, my dears,' said old Mrs. Rabbit one morning, 'you may go into the fields or down the lane, but don't go into Mr. McGregor's garden: your father had an accident there; he was put in a pie by Mrs. McGregor.'

Once upon a time there were four little rabbits, and their names were —

Flopsy,

Mopsy,

Cotton-tail,

and Peter.

Then old Mrs. Rabbit took a basket and her umbrella, and went through the wood to the baker's. She bought a loaf of brown bread and five currant buns.

'Now run along, and don't get into mischief. I am going out.'

But Peter, who was very naughty, ran straight away to Mr. McGregor's garden, and squeezed under the gate!

Flopsy, Mopsy, and Cotton-tail, who were good little bunnies, went down the lane to gather blackberries:

First he ate some lettuces
and some French beans; and
then he ate some radishes;
  And then, feeling rather
sick, he went to look for some
parsley.

Mr. McGregor was on his hands and knees planting out young cabbages, but he jumped up and ran after Peter, waving a rake and calling out, 'Stop thief!'

But round the end of a cucumber frame, whom should he meet but Mr. McGregor!

Peter was most dreadfully frightened; he rushed all over the garden, for he had forgotten the way back to the gate.

He lost one of his shoes among the cabbages, and the other shoe amongst the potatoes.

After losing them, he ran on four legs and went faster, so that I think he might have got away altogether if he had not unfortunately run into a gooseberry net, and got caught by the large buttons on his jacket. It was a blue jacket with brass buttons, quite new.

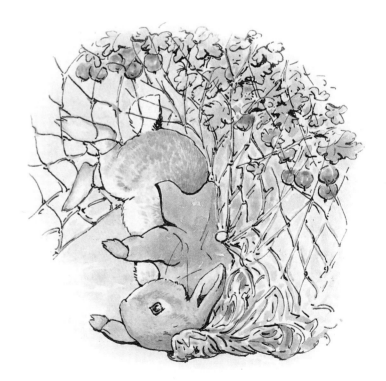

Mr. McGregor came up with a sieve, which he intended to pop upon the top of Peter; but Peter wriggled out just in time, leaving his jacket behind him.

Peter gave himself up for lost, and shed big tears; but his sobs were overheard by some friendly sparrows, who flew to him in great excitement, and implored him to exert himself.

And rushed into the tool-shed, and jumped into a can. It would have been a beautiful thing to hide in, if it had not had so much water in it.

Mr. McGregor was quite sure that Peter was somewhere in the tool-shed, perhaps hidden underneath a flower-pot. He began to turn them over carefully, looking under each.

Presently Peter sneezed – 'Kertyschoo!' Mr. McGregor was after him in no time.

And tried to put his foot upon Peter, who jumped out of a window, upsetting three plants. The window was too small for Mr. McGregor, and he was tired of running after Peter. He went back to his work.

Peter sat down to rest; he was out of breath and trembling with fright, and he had not the least idea which way to go. Also he was very damp with sitting in that can.

After a time he began to wander about, going lippity — lippity — not very fast, and looking all round.

He found a door in a wall; but it was locked, and there was no room for a fat little rabbit to squeeze underneath.

An old mouse was running in and out over the stone doorstep, carrying peas and beans to her family in the wood. Peter asked her the way to the gate, but she had such a large pea in her mouth that she could not answer. She only shook her head at him. Peter began to cry.

Then he tried to find his way straight across the garden, but he became more and more puzzled.

Presently, he came to a pond where Mr. McGregor filled his water-cans. A white cat was staring at some gold-fish, she sat very, very still, but now and then the tip of her tail twitched as if it were alive. Peter thought it best to go away without speaking to her; he had heard about cats from his cousin, little Benjamin Bunny.

He went back towards the tool-shed, but suddenly, quite close to him, he heard the noise of a hoe — scr-r-ritch, scratch, scratch, scritch. Peter scuttered underneath the bushes.

he saw was Mr. McGregor hoeing onions. His back was turned towards Peter, and beyond him was the gate!

Peter got down very quietly off the wheelbarrow, and started running as fast as he could go, along a straight walk behind some black-currant bushes.

Mr. McGregor caught sight of him at the corner, but Peter did not care. He slipped underneath the gate, and was safe at last in the wood outside the garden.

But presently, as nothing happened, he came out, and climbed upon a wheel-barrow and peeped over. The first thing

clothes. It was the second little jacket and pair of shoes that Peter had lost in a fortnight!

Mr. McGregor hung up the little jacket and the shoes for a scarecrow to frighten the blackbirds.

Peter never stopped running or looked behind him till he got home to the big fir-tree.

He was so tired that he flopped down upon the nice soft sand on the floor of the rabbit-hole and shut his eyes. His mother was busy cooking; she wondered what he had done with his

'One table-spoonful to be taken at bedtime.'

But Flopsy, Mopsy, and Cotton-tail had bread and milk and blackberries for supper.

THE END.

I am sorry to say that Peter was not very well during the evening.

His mother put him to bed, and made some camomile tea; and she gave a dose of it to Peter!

THE TALE OF THE FLOPSY BUNNIES

It is said that the effect of eating too much lettuce is "soporific."

I have never felt sleepy after eating lettuces; but then *I* am not a rabbit.

They certainly had a very soporific effect upon the Flopsy Bunnies!

When Benjamin Bunny grew up, he married his Cousin Flopsy. They had a large family, and they were very improvident and cheerful.

I do not remember the separate names of their children; they were generally called the "Flopsy Bunnies."

Sometimes Peter Rabbit had no cabbages to spare.

As there was not always quite enough to eat, — Benjamin used to borrow cabbages from Flopsy's brother, Peter Rabbit, who kept a nursery garden.

Mr. McGregor's rubbish heap was a mixture. There were jam pots and paper bags, and mountains of chopped grass from the mowing machine (which always tasted oily), and some rotten vegetable marrows and an old boot or two. One day — oh joy! — there were a quantity of overgrown lettuces, which had "shot" into flower.

When this happened, the Flopsy Bunnies went across the field to a rubbish heap, in the ditch outside Mr. McGregor's garden.

The little Flopsy Bunnies slept delightfully in the warm sun. From the lawn beyond the garden came the distant clacketty sound of the mowing machine. The blue-bottles buzzed about the wall, and a little old mouse picked over the rubbish among the jam pots.

(I can tell you her name, she was called Thomasina Tittlemouse, a woodmouse with a long tail.)

The Flopsy Bunnies simply stuffed lettuces. By degrees, one after another, they were overcome with slumber, and lay down in the mown grass.

Benjamin was not so much overcome as his children. Before going to sleep he was sufficiently wide awake to put a paper bag over his head to keep off the flies.

She rustled across the paper bag, and
awakened Benjamin Bunny.

The mouse apologized profusely, and
said that she knew Peter Rabbit.

While she and Benjamin were talking,
close under the wall, they heard a
heavy tread above their heads; and
suddenly Mr. McGregor emptied out a
sackful of lawn mowings right upon
the top of the sleeping Flopsy Bunnies!
Benjamin shrank down under his paper
bag. The mouse hid in a jam pot.

The little rabbits smiled sweetly in
their sleep under the shower of grass;
they did not awake because the lettuces
had been so soporific.

They dreamt that their mother
Flopsy was tucking them up in a hay
bed.

Mr. McGregor looked down after
emptying his sack. He saw some funny
little brown tips of ears sticking up
through the lawn mowings. He stared
at them for some time.

"One, two, three, four! five! six leetle rabbits!" said he as he dropped them into his sack.

The Flopsy Bunnies dreamt that their mother was turning them over in bed. They stirred a little in their sleep, but still they did not wake up.

Presently a fly settled on one of them and it moved.

Mr. McGregor climbed down on to the rubbish heap —

(who had remained at home) came across the field.

She looked suspiciously at the sack and wondered where everybody was?

Mr. McGregor tied up the sack and left it on the wall.

He went to put away the mowing machine.

While he was gone, Mrs. Flopsy Bunny

Then the mouse came out of her jam pot, and Benjamin took the paper bag off his head, and they told the doleful tale.

Benjamin and Flopsy were in despair, they could not undo the string.

But Mrs. Tittlemouse was a resourceful person. She nibbled a hole in the bottom corner of the sack.

Their parents stuffed the empty sack with three rotten vegetable marrows, an old blacking-brush and two decayed turnips.

Then they all hid under a bush and watched for Mr. McGregor.

The little rabbits were pulled out and pinched to wake them.

Mr. McGregor came
back and picked up
the sack, and carried
it off.

He carried it hanging
down, as if it were
rather heavy.

The Flopsy Bunnies
followed at a safe
distance.

Mr. McGregor threw down the sack on the stone floor in a way that would have been extremely painful to the Flopsy Bunnies, if they had happened to have been inside it.

They could hear him drag his chair on the flags, and chuckle —

"One, two, three, four, five, six leetle rabbits!" said Mr. McGregor.

"Eh? What's that? What have they been spoiling now?" enquired Mrs. McGregor.

"One, two, three, four, five, six leetle fat

They watched him go into his house. And then they crept up to the window to listen.

rabbits!" repeated Mr. McGregor, counting on his fingers — "one, two, three — "

"Don't you be silly; what do you mean, you silly old man?"

"In the sack! one, two, three, four, five, six!" replied Mr. McGregor.

(The youngest Flopsy Bunny got upon the window-sill.)

Mrs. McGregor took hold of the sack and felt it. She said she could feel six, but they must be *old* rabbits, because they were so hard and all different shapes.

"Not fit to eat; but the skins will do fine to line my old cloak."

"Line your old cloak?" shouted Mr. McGregor — "I shall sell them and buy myself baccy!"

"Rabbit tobacco! I shall skin them and cut off their heads."

And Mr. McGregor was very angry too. One of the rotten marrows came flying through the kitchen window, and hit the youngest Flopsy Bunny.

It was rather hurt.

Mrs. McGregor untied the sack and put her hand inside.

When she felt the vegetables she became very very angry. She said that Mr. McGregor had "done it a purpose".

Then Benjamin and
Flopsy thought that it
was time to go home.

So Mr. McGregor did not get his tobacco, and Mrs. McGregor did not get her rabbit skins.

But next Christmas Thomasina Tittlemouse got a present of enough rabbit-wool to make herself a cloak and a hood, and a handsome muff and a pair of warm mittens.

THE END.